by AJ Ster

illustrated by Doreen Mulryan Marts

Grosset & Dunlap
An Imprint of Penguin Group (USA) Inc.

For Nina, of course.—AJS

Thanks as always to everyone at Penguin: Francesco Sedita, Bonnie Bader, Caroline Sun, Scottie Bowditch, and my editor, Jordan Hamessley, and also, of course, to Doreen Mulryan Marts, who draws Frannie just like I'd pictured her. Your support and enthusiasm is unparalleled! To Julie Barer, who negotiates like nobody's business and to my family and friends for their support. And of course to my nieces and nephews: Maisie, Mia, Lili, Adam, and Nathan, without whom I'd have lost touch long ago with the bane and beauty of kid linguistics.—AJS

GROSSET & DUNLAP
Published by the Penguin Group
Penguin Group (USA) Inc., 375 Hudson Street, New York, New York 10014, USA
Penguin Group (Canada), 90 Eglinton Avenue East, Suite 700, Toronto,
Ontario M4P 2Y3, Canada (a division of Pearson Penguin Canada Inc.)
Penguin Books Ltd., 80 Strand, London WC2R 0RL, England
Penguin Group Ireland, 25 St. Stephen's Green, Dublin 2, Ireland
(a division of Penguin Books Ltd.)
Penguin Group (Australia), 250 Camberwell Road, Camberwell, Victoria 3124,
Australia (a division of Pearson Australia Group Pty. Ltd.)
Penguin Books India Pvt. Ltd., 11 Community Centre,
Panchsheel Park, New Delhi—110 017, India
Penguin Group (NZ), 67 Apollo Drive, Rosedale, Auckland 0632, New Zealand
(a division of Pearson New Zealand Ltd.)
Penguin Books (South Africa) (Pty.) Ltd., 24 Sturdee Avenue,
Rosebank, Johannesburg 2196, South Africa

Penguin Books Ltd., Registered Offices: 80 Strand, London WC2R 0RL, England



Library of Congress Control Number: 2011018038

ISBN 978-0-448-45544-0 (pbk)
ISBN 978-0-448-45545-7 (hc)

10 9 8 7 6 5 4 3 2
10 9 8 7 6 5 4 3 2 1

# CHAPTER

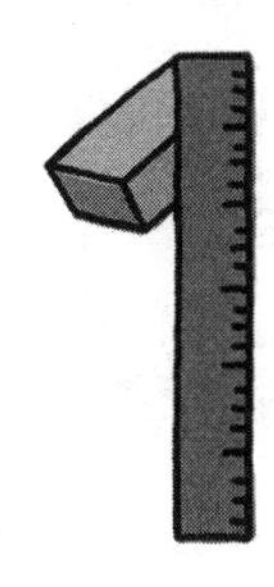

My day started out so perfect I knew that nothing could go wrong. When I got downstairs for breakfast, my dad told me we'd run out of eggs and asked if I'd mind waffles. Or pancakes. Or **BOTH**. After he made me both and laid the plate down in front of my face, he went to get the powdered sugar. Powdered sugar is my favorite. He **tip-topped** it over the pancakes while looking at the paper and was so **distractified**, too much came out! Then, when he poured the syrup for me, the cap was loose and lots of syrup came out. It was the **sugariest** kind of breakfast. That is how my day started out. Sweet and not even one bit sour.

Even my mom was in a good mood. She drove me to school whistling. Usually she was grumpy in the morning until the very last sip of her first cup of coffee. Today she had only four sips! What was happening to these people? And at school, when I reached my classroom, I saw Mrs. Pellington, and she had a really secret smile inside her face. I'm very smart about **secret, inside-face smiles**. She clapped her hands together to get our attention, and we clapped back to tell her we were attentioned.

"Elliott, face forward. Frannie, put your briefcase away. Millicent, put your book down," Mrs. Pellington said. Millicent was always reading. She hid books on her lap, and sometimes she hid her books inside other books. I've even seen her walk into walls. That's how much Millicent loves to read.

"You are not going to want to miss this," Mrs. Pellington said, clapping her hands right off her arms.

Every year our school has a bake sale to raise money for itself. It's a really fun day, and next to our school fair, it's the one day I look forward to the most. So when Mrs. Pellington started out her special announcement by saying, "As you all know, in one week we are supposed to have our annual bake sale," I was very **excitified**. But when she added, "However, it has come to my attention that this year it will not be taking place," my ears were so **shocktified** that tears almost spilled out of them. This was the worst news in the history of forever. It was the opposite of exciting. It was **tragical** is what it was, and that is not an opinion.

But then she continued, "Instead, this year we're going to do something entirely different, but no less wonderful. Children . . . ," she said, getting very quiet so that things got **suspensiful**, "we're going to put on a fashion show!"

That is when everyone in my class went into an uproar, and Mrs. Pellington was so happy, she didn't even clap at our faces for quiet.

"It will be a mother-daughter fashion show with special backstage jobs for the boys," she said, which was the exact sentence that almost made my head fall off. It is a scientific fact that I have always wanted to be in a fashion show with my mother, even if it was something I had never known I'd wanted until **just that second**.

Mrs. Pellington explained that the fashions we'd be wearing were made by local designers and that all the clothes we modeled would be for sale. Everyone would be wearing a different designer. They hoped to match the right outfit with the right girl.

I loved the idea of wearing something that matched me. I try to do it every single day. When I have to be professional and carry my résumé and business cards, I wear something that matches me at the office. (If you don't already know this about me, I am very interested in jobs.) Other times, I pick out regular clothes that suit me really perfectly. I love clothes that you can be **run-aroundy** in. I am not so interested in bows and things that are very shiny. And I do not like pink!

I wondered if there was a designer in town who made business suits. If there was, then she could make me a very professional suit, just like the one my dad wears every day. I would even like a tie to go with it. If I could have a business suit in just my size, I would be the happiest person that ever existed. I looked over at my best friend, Elliott, who could read all of my brain notes, and he gave me the biggest, **worldwide** smile of ever.

"There will be an audition," Mrs. Pellington explained. That sentence made my stomach hurt because maybe the dream I'd had of being in a fashion show with my mother wasn't going to come true.

“Everyone will get the chance to walk down the runway in front of the designers. But not everyone will get picked for the show,” Mrs. Pellington continued.

“What about the people who don’t want to be in the fashion show?” Elizabeth Sanders asked.

Everyone turned to look at her.

Elizabeth Sanders didn't want to be in a fashion show? That did not seem right. Even Mrs. Pellington agreed because she asked, "You don't want to be in the fashion show, Elizabeth?"

"Well, I do, but my mother said she wouldn't be here for the bake sale. And if the fashion show is instead of the bake sale, then my mom won't be here!" She sounded very **upsettish**.

"Perhaps you can help with hair and makeup," Mrs. Pellington offered. Elizabeth's eyes almost **flew out of her head**, that's how excitified she was at this sentence. I wasn't so interested in hair and makeup, so I didn't feel worried about not getting a job like that.

"I would love that job, Mrs. Pellington. Thank you very much."

"What are the backstage jobs for boys?" Elliott said, looking a little worried.

Mrs. Pellington said with a big smile on her face, "The boys are going to help the designers backstage. You are going to be assistant fashion designers."

"Fashion designers?!" Henry called out. "That's for girls!"

"That's not what Zac Posen, Marc

Jacobs, or Michael Kors would say," Mrs. P. told Henry.

"Who are they?" he wanted to know.

"Some of the world's most famous *male* fashion designers," she told him.

"Oh," said Henry, looking **impresstified**. Some of the boys still looked a little confusified, even Elliott. Since Elliott and I are best friends and can read each other's brain notes, I knew that he wasn't exactly perfectly sure what a fashion designer even did. Neither did I, as a matter of fact. We only knew it was a very important job because Mrs. P. said, "It's a very important job."

After her announcement, she said we were going to move on to math, but anyone interested in being in the fashion show should discuss it with their mothers and stay after school tomorrow for the audition. Even though I'd never had one before, I knew that I loved auditions. They were something that grown-ups did, so they were very official and important. I couldn't wait. I was going to bring my briefcase.

I did not love math, **however and nevertheless**, which is why I had a hard time listening. I watched myself inside my brain being the most **workerish** kind of fashion model in the entire world of America. I was going to be the only model alive who carried a briefcase!

# CHAPTER

When I got home from school that day, my legs ran all around the house looking for my mother. When I finally found her cleaning all the cobwebs out from the corners in the basement, I was so out of breath I could barely make a sentence without **gasping my head off**.

I told her all about the fashion show, the local designers, how Elizabeth was helping with hair and makeup, and how the boys were going to be fashion designers. Right before the best part, which I was saving for last because it's a scientific fact that's what you do with the best parts, my heart got very **thumpish**. What if my mother didn't even want to be in a fashion show?

"I can't believe my daughter is going to be a model!" my mother said. "I'm so proud."

"Do you want to be a model, too?" I asked, sending her a brain note from my eyeballs that told her to say, *"Yes, yes I do!!!"* When my mother's own eyeballs got wide, I knew my message had reached her. And when I saw very small smiles on top of her eyeballs, I knew she'd ask to audition **right now**. She might even make them open the school back up for her tonight, that's how badly she wanted to audition! I'm

**very smart** about eyeball smiles and auditions.

"Me?" she asked with a hand over her mouth.

"It's a mother-daughter fashion show! Isn't that exciting?" I cried. My mother stood up and wiped the basement dirt off her hands and onto her beat-up pair of corduroys.

"I've never come out of a department store dressing room, much less walked down a runway."

"There's a first time for everything," I told her, which is a for instance of an expression I took from my dad.

"I guess there is," she said. "But I don't know, Frannie. I'm not wild about the idea."

That is when my heart fell out of its pocket and dropped to the floor and broke into a **hundredy disappointment pieces**.

"It's not a for sure thing yet," I told her. "There's an audition."

That's when she groaned. "An audition? Oh, Frannie—I don't think so."

"Please, Mom! It will be so much fun. Don't you want to work with me? I've always wanted to work with you. It's been my entire lifelong dream since this morning. We could be coworkers! Haven't you always wanted to do that?"

That's when her face grew my favorite type of smile ever, and she said, "Yes, Frannie. In fact, that would be a dream come true for me, too."

"So you'll do it? You'll audition?"

"I'll audition," she said.

Then I jumped up and down, and all my happiness **boggled** around inside.

"You know that fashion models have to walk a certain way down the runway, don't you?" she asked me. My mom knew how **workerish** I was, so that is why she asked me whether I knew. It's a scientific fact that I've had so many jobs, she's probably lost count. Which meant she didn't even remember if I'd been a fashion model before or not. If I had, then I'd have known what exactly she was talking about, actually.

I shook my head no. I was very **impresstified** that my mother was an expert on modeling.

"It's true. They put one foot directly in front of the other and walk, leading with their hips," she explained, demonstrating by walking **weirdier** than anyone I've ever seen in my **worldwide** life.

"Now you try," she told me. I put one foot right in front of the other.

"Now jut your hips out," she said. I jutted my hips out.

"Now throw your shoulders back and lift your chin up."

There were so many instructions, I didn't know how anyone remembered to do all these things at the same time! If my chin was lifted, how could I see where I was going? It was much harder to do than it sounds.

That is why we practiced. Practicing is good because it means you'll get better at something. I love to practice things oftenly so that I can get really good and then go get a job doing those things.

Since we were in the basement, my mom decided it might be fun to open an old box of her clothes from the olden age and wear them as our model outfits.

She found a really good box and opened it, and you will not even **believe your ears** about the clothes she pulled out. She had corduroy skirts, moccasins, braided belts, overalls, painter's pants, crinkled-up jumpsuits, cowboy boots, puffer vests, denim vests, leather vests, something called a peasant shirt that had puffy sleeves, plaid shirts, and a mood ring! Rainbow suspenders, satin jackets, lots of T-shirts with iron-on decals on them, crazy pants that flared out at the bottom, and shirts that were flowish and flowery. She had lots of things called ponchos, which is a for instance of a type of cape that was for fashion and not for superheroes.

I put on the pants with the flares, and tied the braided belt tight so the pants wouldn't fall off. Then I put on a

T-shirt with a decal of something that said SATURDAY NIGHT FEVER. I piled a bunch of rope bracelets onto my wrists, slung a jean purse over my shoulder, and slipped on a pair of shoes with heels made out of corkboards!

When I tried to walk, I couldn't because I don't know how to walk in shoes that are too big and too high. I took them off and did the walk barefoot. I guess I was already an expert because my mom clapped her hands and cried, "Bravo!"

Then she took a turn, and we were having so much fun, we decided to go upstairs where there was much more space. We walked back and forth down our long hall, making each other laugh with made-up walks. One time my mom skipped. Another time she crawled. One time I walked on my tiptoes, and another time I walked backward. We were laughing so hard that we **fell to the ground**, and that is when my dad came home.

"Who are you, and what did you do with my wife and daughter?" he asked us both.

"Daddy, it's us!" I said, jumping up. "We're wearing Mom's old clothes, and we're modeling!"

"Modeling! Wow. I didn't know you were interested in modeling, Frannie," my dad told me, putting down his briefcase and taking off his business jacket.

"Well, I wasn't. Not until today, at least. My school is putting on a fashion show for mothers and daughters," I told him. "You have to audition, though. So it's not a scientific fact yet that we'll be models."

My dad looked very **impresstified** by everything I'd just said.

"This is the most exciting thing to happen all day," my dad said.

"Isn't it?" my mom said. "Frannie and I might get to work together."

"Well, now I'm jealous," he said, and that is when **my whole face blushed right up**. I never knew my dad wanted to work with me! That filled me up with so much **pride-itity**.

"Don't worry, Dad. I bet there will be a father-daughter fashion show one day, and we could do that together."

My mom and dad laughed, but I don't know why. They were probably just really happy that they were going to have jobs with their daughter. Maybe it was their dream since this morning, too.

"Perhaps, Frannie. Either way, I feel very lucky living with two of the most beautiful girls in Chester, New York," my dad told us.

My mother and I looked at each other and smiled. We were very proud of ourselves, even if we weren't quite sure why.

# CHAPTER

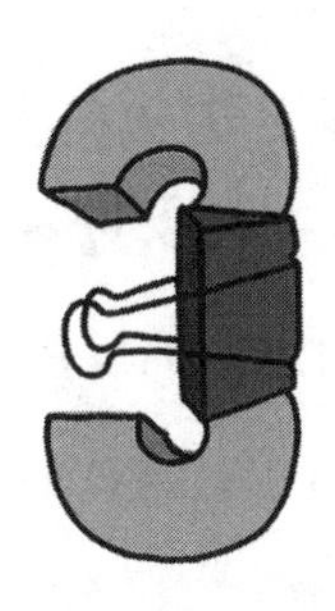

On audition day, I woke up with moths and butterflies in my stomach. I could not believe the nerves **surfboarding** around inside me! Even my mother was nervous. She told me so at breakfast.

"Even if you don't make it," my dad told us, "you two will always be models in my eyes."

That gave us both big smiles, and my mom mussed his hair up and kissed him. "Oh, Dan. You big flatterer, you."

Although I didn't know exactly what that meant, I smiled at him because I knew it was nice.

Once I got to school, my smile muscles weren't working so well. All the moths and butterflies were making me very nervous. Instead of being **concentratey** on school like I was supposed to be, I was just **concentratey** on the audition like I was not supposed to be. I don't have enough fingers to count the times Mrs. P. clapped in my direction because I wasn't paying attention.

"I know you're very excited for today's audition, but you need to be where you are and not where you're not, all right, Frannie?" Mrs. P. said to me.

"All right, Mrs. P.," I told her. "But I

can't promise it will work." Which was the truth of the world.

Finally, when I really thought that maybe the day would never, ever get to three o'clock, that this would be the one day in history where it never turned three o'clock, it turned three o'clock! That is when I grabbed my briefcase and followed the other auditioning girls to the auditorium. I thought my eyes were going to pop out of my brain sockets when I saw how many people were there. I saw my mom sitting in the third row, and she waved and pointed to the empty seat she had saved right beside her.

I could not even believe my eyes about what they had done to the auditorium, practically overnight. Instead of the long aisle we walked down to get to our seats, they'd built a long pier, with no lake at the end of it. I didn't know what piers had to do with modeling.

There was a **sign-in sheet** where you had to write your name if you were auditioning. I didn't know if this was part of the audition or not, so I wrote in my best script, Mrs. Frankly B. Miller, just in case. Frankly is what I'm called when I have jobs. Otherwise, I'm just plain Frannie.

Elliott and Elizabeth found me and my mother and slid in with us. They said they were going to clap the hardest for me and Millicent because we were their friends and it might win us the best outfits. Soon, a woman in a sweatshirt and torn jeans came and stood in front of us. She was yelling at us to get our attention, but we didn't respond to yellers, only clappers. That is why Mrs. Pellington got up and stood next to the woman and clapped her hands and we got quiet.

"Please listen to Laura. She has very important instructions for you to follow."

"Hi, everyone. My name is Laura Munn."

"Hi, Laura Munn!" we yelled back at her starting-to-smile face.

"I am producing the fashion show at your school. All of the designers are very honored and excited to donate their fashions, and we have wonderful designs to choose from. My job is to choose the best mother-daughter pairs for the clothes the designers have made. I clearly have my work cut out for me because when I look out at the audience, I see so many beautiful people. Today, you are going to learn how to walk like a model from a top professional."

That is when I turned to my mom, and we gave each other smiles about this sentence. Mine was a **double smile** about knowing how to model walk and also about learning from a *professional*!

"So I will turn it over to Mia Rubel, who trains models how to walk down the catwalk."

Everyone started looking at one another very **confusified**. Catwalk? But before we had time to even ask that question with our mouths, a very tall, beautiful, blond woman walked like an ostrich down the runway. She marched all the way to the end, looked out at everyone with a big smile, turned, and then walked back like she was late for a very important meeting. A minute later, she returned and sat on the end of the stage to stare at us.

"Hi to every one of you beautiful girls."

"Hi," we all said back (even the moms said hi back, and it's a scientific fact they are not girls anymore).

"As you just saw, models have very specific walks. What I just demonstrated was the way I'd like all of you to walk."

There were a lot of gasp sounds.

"When Laura calls your name, you'll get your photo taken, then you'll climb up to the catwalk and give us your best walk."

Laura Munn called out Millicent and

Monica, her mom, and we clapped for them. Laura stopped her at the foot of the stage and took a Polaroid picture of each of them. Then she handed the picture to another girl who shook it out and then wrote MILLICENT in black ink across the bottom of Millicent's photo and MONICA across her mom's. I was so **jealous** of that girl. The assistant stapled the picture to a piece of paper and handed it back to Laura, who wrote on it while Millicent clomped down the catwalk. We clapped

really hard for her because she was our friend. At the end of the runway, Millicent stood for a **millisecond** of a meter, then turned and went back to her seat.

"Fantastic!" Laura Munn called out. "Next!" And then Millicent's mom, Monica, had her turn.

I did not appreciate how little time Millicent and Monica spent on the stage. They did not even stand for longer than a breath when they got to the end of the catwalk. What was fantastic about spending no time on a job like that? When I got to the end of the stage, I was going to stand there for much longer than one half of a **secondteen** second. What kind of job lasted so short? Not any job I wanted! I was much more serious about jobs than

Millicent and her mom, and that is not an opinion.

"I am getting really nervous," my mom leaned over to tell me.

"Don't worry, Mom! Just be yourself!" I told her, which is a for instance of something she would have said to me.

Right after I said that, Laura Munn called our names, and moths flew up all around my belly again. I picked up my briefcase, and we walked over to Laura Munn.

Everyone was clapping for us, and we weren't even on the stage yet!

My mom went first. After she got her picture taken, she walked up to the stage and did the most perfect model walk she'd ever done. When she finished, Laura Munn told her, "That was excellent, thank you." My mom blushed and whispered in my eardrum, "Go get 'em, tiger," which made me feel amazing.

After I got my picture taken, you will not believe the horrible thing Laura Munn said: "You can't carry that briefcase on the runway."

I was **horrendified** by this sentence. This was not something I preferred.

"Why not?" I asked.

"Because it's not part of the show."

"But modeling is a job, and this is my job, and I carry a briefcase to all my jobs," I told her, which made her smile but did not change her mind.

"I'm very sorry. Modeling isn't that kind of a job."

I scrunched up my face at this sentence, and that is when I had my first wondering about this career. I was not sure that modeling was a very good job for someone like me.

I put my briefcase down, then climbed the stairs to the catwalk, which is a for instance of what the professionals call the runway.

I did my walk even better than I did at home, and when I got to the end, I did not turn quickly to head back like everyone else had. I stopped and smiled and waved and twirled and curtsied, and just when I was about to bow, Laura got **interruptish** and told me to hurry back. Laura didn't work at this school, so she didn't know how **offendish** this was to me. I was probably the most **workerish** person she'd ever worked with, and she just thought I was a kid. If she knew how professional I was, then she never would have told me to hurry back. She would have appreciated how long I stood at the end of the stage. She would have understood that what I was doing was working.

When I got off the stage, Laura

called me over and told me that during the real show, I was to count to three and then quickly turn around and come back. She said I could not stand on the end of the stage for more than three seconds.

*Three?* What kind of a terrible job was being a model? Three seconds wasn't even working. That didn't even count as a job.

"That's not a very long time," I said.

"No, it's not. Being a runway model is fast-paced work, and it goes by very quickly."

I do not like fast-paced work that goes by quickly. I like jobs that take a lot of time. I wondered how long Elliott's job would take. Probably an entire day. I was starting to wonder if I was auditioning for the wrong job. I went and sat back down next to my mom, who said I was very **fantastical**.

Elliott and Elizabeth each gave me big smiles and a thumbs-up and mouthed the word *awesome*. Then we watched the rest of the mothers and daughters take their turns.

At the end of the audition, Laura said we all did very well, and that they would be deciding tonight which outfit we'd each be wearing. We were to come back at the same time the day after tomorrow, and we'd try on our dresses.

**Dresses?** I did not realize that I was going to have to wear a dress. I am not really a dress kind of a person, but maybe because the audition was to match us to the dress, they knew I was not a flowery and pink dress type of girl. Those were not the kinds of dresses I preferred. Maybe it was a business suit dress. I did not love that, either, but it was the best type of dress I could think of to wear. Or a **sweatshirt dress**. That would be good, too.

Then I heard my dad's voice knocking in my head. "One step at a time, Frannie," it said. Which is a for instance of, don't make plans you don't yet have.

# CHAPTER

The next morning, I walked into school and saw a clump of kids staring at the wall. Elliott was in the back of the clump trying to get in, but it wasn't working. When he saw me he was so excited he blurted out, "They're up, Frannie! They're up!" which was exciting, except I didn't know what he was talking about.

"What's up?"

"The audition pages. The people who

are going to be in the fashion show—they're up!"

That's when the moths and butterflies flew back into my stomach, and I inched forward as people turned and left the clump either happy or sad with the news.

When I finally got to the front, I looked at the page, but I was so nervous that the letters took a really long time to even make sense to me. Which is a for instance of why it took me **seventy-five years** to see that I was listed as number six. I was so happy, I almost hugged Elliott, which is not something I normally do in public.

"I made it!" I told him.

"I knew you would. You were the best model up there. Everyone else was much too fast, but not you," he said.

This is why Elliott and I are best friends. He understands the important things in the world, like how jobs should take a long time and that short jobs do not feel very official.

"Thanks, Elliott!"

Millicent got a part in the fashion show, too, but I worried she wouldn't be able to put down her book long enough to walk the runway.

The show was all anyone could talk about all day long. All the teachers were annoyed, not just Mrs. Pellington. If you listened carefully, you could hear our school **clapping its head off** trying to get everyone's attention inside. Everyone was excited for the day to end so we could go home and tell our moms! My mom was not going to believe her own ear sockets about this news!

And I was right. She said she was thrilled and couldn't wait until the next day when we got "fitted" for our outfits. *Fitted* is a for instance of a word that means "trying on dresses."

Even though I didn't like dresses very much, I started to get excited to see mine. Laura Munn told everyone that we'd be wearing dresses she thought matched who we were.

This was a very interesting thing to me. I was very curious to see what kind of dress she thought I was. I could tell, because Laura Munn wore sneakers, jeans, and sweatshirts, that she knew I was the same type of person as her. And that is why I stopped being so scared about what kind of a dress she chose. I fell asleep with visions of business suit dresses dancing in my head.

The next day, after almost **two thousand hours** of school, Millicent and I ran down to the auditorium to meet our moms. We stood in a line while Laura and her assistant handed out long bags to everyone with our dresses zipped up inside them. Backstage there were mirrors and privacy, and that's where everyone went to try theirs on. My mom hung my bag up next to hers so that we could unzip our bags at the same time.

"Ready?" she asked me.

I nodded my head yes.

"Set? Unzip!" she called, and we both unzipped at the same time, and we both gasped at the same time, and then at the same time, we both spoke out loud. "Oh, wow!" she said.

And I said, "Oh no!"

My eyes were **shocktified** by what they saw: flowers. Pink flowers. I could not believe it. Laura Munn, the one fashion person I thought would understand who I was, clearly did not understand me one bit!

"Oh, they're beautiful. Aren't they beautiful, Frannie?" my mom cried.

No, I wanted to say. They are not beautiful. They are very flowerish and girly, and it is a scientific fact that **I am not flowerish and girly**, but that is a rude thing to say, so instead I didn't say anything.

My mom was already trying on her dress. And to think, just two days ago she didn't really want to do this at all and I did. Now it was the other way around. When she was finished zipping up, she turned to look at me, and she really did look actually amazing. That is a for instance of why I gasped in a big gulp of air and said, "Wow, Mom. You look beautiful."

"Thank you, Frannie. Now, try yours on. I want to see how it looks on you." Which was something I did not want to see. But I did it, anyway, because it's a scientific fact I didn't have much choice. When I was done, I looked in the full-length mirror, and my mom stood behind me to look at me.

"Oh, Frannie, you are stunning. Simply beautiful."

My mom's eyeballs must have broken off their sockets because I did not look stunning or simply beautiful. I looked like a **disgusting** and awful flower store.

# CHAPTER

Laura and her assistant walked around **oohing** and **aahing** at how good everyone looked in their dresses. She walked over to me and my mom.

"Oh, you both look fabulous!" Laura told us. My mom thanked her, and I **harrumphed**. "Are you ready to go through hair and makeup now?" she asked us.

Hair and makeup?

"Oh, how fun!" my mom said.

I did not want anyone doing my hair or putting **one ounce** of makeup on my face. This is not the type of girl I am at all.

I looked over and saw Elizabeth laughing and holding brushes and bobby pins, which looked much more exciting than wearing a flower dress.

And Elliott was helping with hanging things up, and the other boys were rolling lint brushes over things. I was so jealous of all of them.

There were a couple of other people who were part of Laura Munn's "team," who were putting stickpins in people's dresses and using chalk to draw on them all over the place.

I even saw someone take scissors and cut some strings off. This was a very interesting part of modeling that I did not know about. I liked drawing and cutting things much more than I liked modeling things. I wondered what that job was called because that seemed like a job I would love.

The woman doing the cutting and drawing called Elliott over, and she handed him the chalk and scissors to hold. Elliott was the **luckiest** person I'd ever known. He had the best job in the entire universe. It was the only time I ever wanted to be his assistant.

Then Laura and her assistant talked about us like we were not there. They said the **weirdiest** things like, "I think we should play up her eyes, and let's add some texture to her hair. Did we remember to bring the dry shampoo?"

*Dry shampoo?* I had never even heard of such a thing. Then one of them ran over to Elizabeth, and she showed her a bottle of something that must have been dry shampoo. Elizabeth Sanders knew about dry shampoo and I didn't? What else was there to know? I had to work backstage. It was so much better than walking down the runway.

Laura started picking up sections of my hair, twirling it around, and discussing how to make my hair "work." This was very **confusifying**.

Was my hair going to get a job? Hair couldn't work, could it? Then Laura brought me over to the hair person.

"My name is Delilah, and I'm so excited to do your hair to match your beautiful dress," she said. No one could have said anything more **worse** to me in my entire lifetime.

I did not want her to make my hair match my dress. I reached out and grabbed Elizabeth's hand and squeezed it. She understood all about me, and she said, "Don't worry, Frannie. It's only for one day. It will be over really quickly."

I nodded, but even one day with flowers all over myself felt too long.

Delilah was the **meanest** person I'd ever met because of what she did to my hair. A for instance of what I mean is that she put a lot of flowers in my hair. I thought a hair person made your hair better, not worse! So far, being a model was the **worst job** I ever had and the only one I wanted to quit.

When Delilah put flowers in my mother's hair, my mom was very happy because she is much more girly than I am. Then I went into makeup. Elizabeth asked if she could come with me, and Delilah told her yes.

The makeup person was a man, which was why he didn't know how to put on makeup. Kevin painted my entire face with cream, then fluffed my cheeks up with powder, and then wiped pink smudge on my cheeks and slicked the rest of the pink onto my lips.

When he was done, my face felt heavy, like he drew a whole other face on top of the face I already had. When I looked at myself, that's when I really felt like I had another face on my face. I hardly recognized who I was!

My face looked like it wanted to be **a clown**, and my hair looked like it fell into **a flower garden**.

I could feel the tears rolling up the inside of my head toward my eyeballs. I tried to suck all my tears back into my head before they spilled out all over the place.

I was very **humilified** to be seen wearing this outfit and having makeup on my face and flowers in my hair. This was not who I was, and I did not want to show myself to everyone in the world wearing things I would never in a million years wear. I did not want to be a model at all. And I did not appreciate that Laura Munn thought I matched pink and flower things!

"Oh, you look marvelous!" Laura said when she saw me.

I knew I was supposed to smile and say thank you because that is polite, so that is what I made my face do.

"All right, everyone," Laura said. "This is what you're going to look like for the show tomorrow. I hope you all like it. Take care of your outfits. You are in charge of them. Tomorrow, you will eat dinner in the cafeteria at five PM. Please arrive here by six PM and not one second later. The show will start at seven PM on the nose. All right?"

"All right!" we all yelled back and then changed out of our **ugly** dresses and put them back into their bag homes. Then I ran out of there and waited for my mother and Elliott. Elliott was eating dinner over at our house, which was the only good thing to happen all day, and it hadn't even happened yet!

# CHAPTER

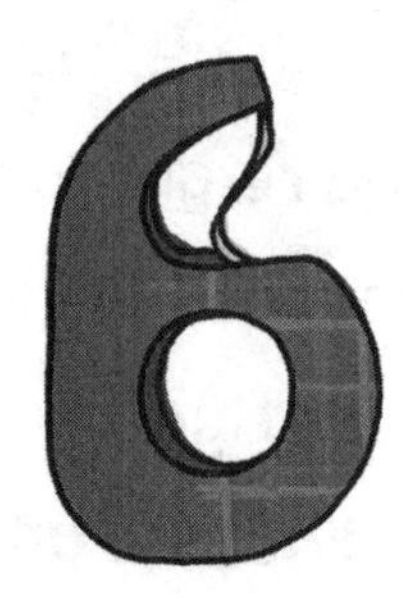

On the car ride home, my mom was **so excited** about the whole thing, she said she wanted to learn how to sew and make clothes herself. That did sound like fun. I would like to make clothes, too. I had lots of ideas all the time, and I was a very good draw-er.

Elliott was telling us about all of the things he learned about being a fashion designer, and the more he said about it, the more interesting it was.

He told us that you could take clothes apart and put them back together if you needed to grow or shrink them. He said you could make anything shorter but only some things longer. He said you could go to any fabric store and pick out your favorite type of fabric and make anything you wanted out of any material.

I looked at my dress hanging on the hook in the car, and all of a sudden, I got some **very good ideas**.

At dinner, my mom and Elliott were busy telling my dad all about their wonderful, glorious jobs, while I was wondering if I might **secretly** be a very good fashion designer. Maybe I had a hidden talent for it. I probably have lots of hidden talents. I just don't know what they are yet.

My dad oohed and aahed at everything they said, and then he turned to me. "You're awfully quiet, Frannie. Don't you like being a model?"

"No," I told him.

This surprised him because he scrunched up his face at this sentence.

"You don't?"

"No. They make you wear ugly dresses, and they dye your face different colors and pour plants on your head, and you have to walk like an ostrich, and you only get to stand at the end of the stage for one half second. It's the worst job I've ever had."

My dad tried not to smile. I could tell. I'm really smart about trying-not-to-smile smiles.

"Sounds terrible."

"It is. It's the worst job in history.

Don't ever be a model, Dad."

"I think I can safely promise you that I won't."

"That's a relief," I told him.

Elliott and I excused ourselves and went to my bedroom where I had a **secret mission** that I had not yet told to Elliott.

My fashion show dress was hanging from a hook on the back of my closet door. I stood in front of it and stared.

"I don't like this dress, Elliott. Not even one little bit," I told him.

"But you looked really pretty in it, Frannie," he said. That made me feel really special inside, but it didn't make me like the dress any more.

"But it doesn't match me. Laura Munn said all of the dresses would match the wearers, but this one doesn't."

Elliott bent his head to the side and stared at the dress and studied it. He was probably looking at it as a fashion designer because that was what he did for a living that week.

"Maybe it's the flowers that don't match," he said.

"It *is* the flowers that don't match! I don't like the flowers, and I don't like that they are pink!"

"There's not really so much you can do. You'll never have to wear it again except for tomorrow night."

"I don't want people to see me in this dress and think it's who I am. It's not who I am at all. If I wear it, it'll be like I am lying, and I don't want to lie at my job!"

"Well, what else is there to do?"

"We can make it match me," I said.

"How?" he asked.

We stared at the dress on its hanger and made scrunched-up faces.

"Got any ideas?" he asked me.

"No. You?" I asked him.

"No," he said. We were stumpified.

"Let's go ask my mom," I said, which he thought was a geniusal idea because he smiled.

Elliott and I went to my mom's room to ask her expert advice, but she wasn't there. We heard the TV, so we went downstairs into the living room, and you will not believe your ears about what my mom was doing. She was watching a show about fashion! On it, people were cutting up clothes and sewing and ripping fabric and running around. They looked like mad people trying to make an outfit before the clock struck midnight. That's what they were doing backstage today, too. That's when I understood that the way to fix clothes was to cut and draw on them! Why in the world didn't I ever think of that myself?

I grabbed Elliott's hand and started to run back to my room.

"But we didn't ask your mom," he said.

"Don't need to," I told him. "I figured it out!"

Upstairs, I took the dress off its hanger and laid it out on the floor.

"First, we have to get rid of the flowers," I told Elliott.

"Do you want to cut them out?" he asked.

I wondered about that, but then realized the dress would be made of holes, and I certainly could not walk down the runway with a **holey** dress. I looked around my room and saw exactly the thing we needed. A magic marker. I ran over to my desk, grabbed a thick, black ink pen, got down on my knees, and started to x out all the flowers.

"Frannie! I don't think you should be doing that!" Elliott cried.

"Elliott, it's okay," I said. "I have hidden talents as a fashion designer."

"You do?"

"Yes."

"I didn't know that. What are they?"

"Well, I don't know yet. But if you don't let me do this, we'll never find out."

Elliott thought about this for a second, and when he decided I was right, he said, "You're right."

After we **x-ed** out all the flowers, I

went and got my scissors.

"What are you going to do with those?" he asked.

"Cut," I told him.

"You're going to cut it?" Elliott's eyeballs looked shocktified.

"Yes. That's how I'm going to fix it. Just like they did on the TV show."

"Do you think that's a good idea?" Elliott asked me.

It was a very good idea, actually and as a matter of fact, so I didn't respond with words to that, I just stared Elliott straight in the eyeballs until he shrugged and watched me cut up the bottom of the dress. When we were done, we stood over it and looked down, but it was very hard to tell if it looked beautiful or just great.

"Put this on," I told Elliott.

"But it's a dress!" he said.

"I know, but I need to see how it looks on someone else in order to know whether my job is done or not."

Elliott rolled his eyes, but he picked up the dress and went to the bathroom to change. I tried not to laugh when he came out wearing the dress, but I couldn't help it, the laugh just fell **right out of my mouth**.

"It's not funny!" Elliott said.

"It's a little funny!"

Then Elliott looked in the mirror and said, "Okay, it is a little funny."

I stood back and stared at the dress, and I will say for a scientific fact that it looked **amazing**.

"What about all these snaggley things hanging down?" Elliott asked, staring at some loose threads that were being born at the bottom of the dress. I loved the **snaggley** things. In fact, I decided that snaggley things would be part of my clothing designs when I was a real-life fashion designer.

"It's a little messy," Elliott said.

It's a scientific fact that he was right. The dress did look a little messy, but I prefer messy to clean, and that is not an opinion.

"You will see hanging threads on all the Messy Miller clothes."

"What's Messy Miller?"

"My clothing line!"

That's when Elliott's eyes almost flew out of their eye sockets.

"Can I work there?"

"Probably. I don't have an office yet. But when I get one, then you can work for me."

This made Elliott very happy.

I stared at the dress again, and while I was very happy with all my *X*s and all the cutoff parts, I was not happy that it was pink. But there wasn't much I could do about that.

I could do something about the shoes, though. A for instance of what I mean is that I did not appreciate the shoes that Laura Munn was making me wear. They were pink and flat, and they were not shoes I would ever make in my Messy Miller business. I knew that shoes were supposed to match their dresses, and that's why she gave me pink shoes. But now the dress had black *X*s on it, and I wanted my shoes to match those.

I looked all over for my rain boots, which matched perfectly. When Elliott put them on, we turned to stare at him in the mirror, and that's when we decided he looked **fabulous**.

I could not wait for the next day. Everyone in the entire world would be so surprised about my secret hidden talents as a fashion designer.

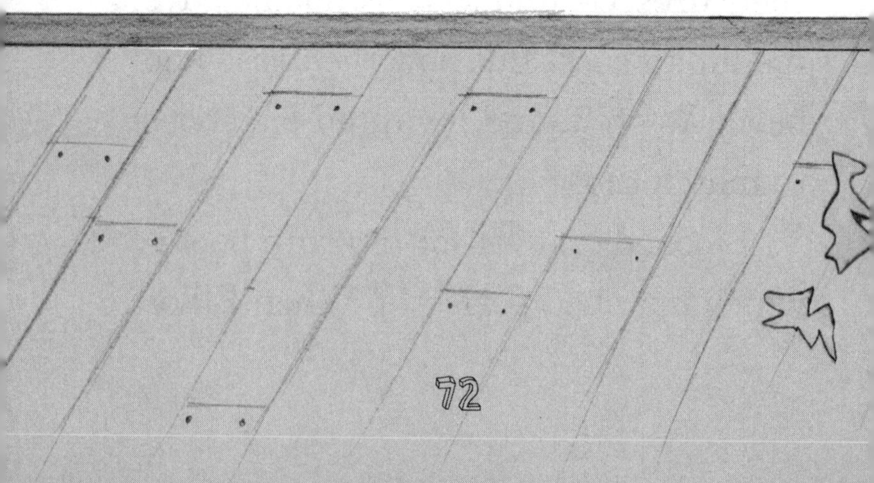

# CHAPTER

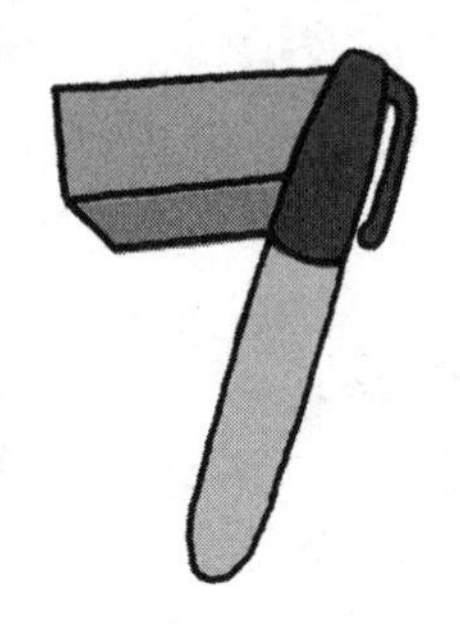

I could not stop imagining how people were going to react when they saw the **fabulous** job I did on my dress. I was going to put on my dress, and before it was time to go on the stage, Laura Munn and the fashion designer who made my dress would see me. They would gasp and clap and cheer and gather everyone around me.

"I had no idea you had a secret hidden talent as a fashion designer,"

Laura Munn would tell me.

"What's your name, little girl?" the fashion designer of the dress would ask.

"Mrs. Frankly B. Miller," I'd tell her.

"Mrs. Miller, I'd like to officially offer you a job working for me. I want you to design all of my clothes, and none of them will be dresses. You are not a model, my dear. You are a natural-born fashion designer."

Then I'd turn to my mother, whose mouth would be ready to fall off her face with **pride-itity** for me, and she'd shake her head in astonishment. "Frannie, I had no idea. No idea at all you were this talented."

I'd shrug and say, "Me neither, but may I please be excused from being a model now? I'd much prefer to make clothes backstage."

"Of course! Of course!" everyone would cry, and then they'd give me my very own station to work at, which would be almost as good as an office! I would put all my supplies for clothes-making in my briefcase, and I would tell everyone to throw away all the makeup and flowers.

My mom would call my dad, and he would come running from work to see me at my new job. Then he'd put his arm around my mom's shoulders, and their eyes would be **blinking** and **wowing** in their eye sockets so hard that you'd actually be able to hear how **impresstified** they were with me. I would be their very own fashion designer daughter of the world.

"Frannie! Frannie!" my mom was saying. I looked up at her, confusified.

"You're in a trance. Try and have a bite of your toast, and then we have to leave for school, okay?" my mom asked.

I looked down at my breakfast plate and was **shocktified** to see that I hadn't even left my house yet. That is how real my imaginary scene felt.

On the drive to school, my mother told me where and when she'd meet me and that she'd bring my dress, and did I zip it back up in the garment bag like she told me to? I nodded yes. Did she need me to bring anything else? I scrunched up my face to think about that sentence. My rain boots were in my briefcase, so she didn't need to bring those.

"I'm all set," I told her.

"Excellent. I'll see you at five for dinner. You can tell me about your day, and then we can go be supermodels."

I kissed her on the cheek and ran out of the car and into school. I did not know how I was going to be patient until five PM.

Mrs. Pellington said that all the models and everyone working

backstage were bringing great pride to the school. This year's event would bring in more money for the school than a bake sale ever had. Then Mrs. Pellington told us that there were going to be some very important people there tonight.

"Like who?" Elizabeth Sanders called out without raising her hand.

"I think there will be a couple of local magazines and the local news channel," she said.

Millicent and I looked at each other with I-cannot-believe-we're-going-to-be-movie-stars eyeballs.

The thing that helps a day go by quickly is when you imagine the amazing things that are going to happen at the very end of the day. I imagined everything I had imagined at breakfast about **ten hundredteen** times, only each time I made the version different. In one of them, I won a very fancy, gold award. In another, I only got a silver award, but I was just as grateful because a bad sport is something my dad told me he never, ever wanted me to be.

When five o'clock finally came, Millicent, Elliott, and I ran to the cafeteria to eat a special early dinner with our parents. Elizabeth ate with us because her mom was out of town. It felt like a special privilege because it was something I had never done before. It's a scientific fact that I love special privileges.

# CHAPTER

After dinner, we had one entire hour before the show. Even though an hour seemed like an awful long time to just put on a dress, my mom explained that everyone had to put on their dresses and get made up and have their hair done. That was when an hour seemed like not enough time at all, as a matter of fact. Funny how time can seem both **long** and **short** at the same time.

There was so much going on

backstage when we got there, I felt a **pang** of upset that we ate our dinner in the cafeteria. If we had eaten backstage, we wouldn't have missed one second of action.

Elliott and Elizabeth ran to their stations, and I felt a little **jealousish** that they got to do such important work. They got to use really grown-up tools, which is a for instance of something I love to use.

Delilah handed Elliott a very professional-looking wand, which she showed him how to work. What it did exactly was blow smoke out of itself and made wrinkles disappear on all the clothes that he wanded it over. It was really cool, and I wanted to try it, but I didn't work at the smoking wand stand. Not yet, anyway.

Elizabeth also got to hold a lot of tools. Delilah let her hold a **hundredy** things at a time. Elizabeth even got to ruffle through the official makeup bag and pull things out. She handed Delilah brushes and potions and bottles, and all of a sudden I wanted to know what else was inside that bag. I felt very envious of Elizabeth that she got to see and touch so many mysterious things.

Laura Munn clapped her hands together and divided everyone up into groups of people. One group had to get dressed and then go into hair and makeup. The other group would go into hair and makeup and then get dressed. I was in the hair and makeup group, and my mom was in the dressed group.

I sat very still while Elizabeth and her boss put all the glop on my face. I didn't even mind or say one word or scrunch up my face or make a bad noise because I knew that after they were done, I was going to wipe it all off. I worried that they might get their feelings hurt, but I knew when they saw how much better I looked without it, their feelings would be the **opposite** of hurt.

I was excited to see how professional-acting Elizabeth was, and I wondered whether she was someone I might have work for me in my fashion designer office. I knew that her résumé would be very impressive now because she had done an actual fashion show. I was very **impresstified** with her, indeed. She held all of the different brushes and smudgers, and when her boss asked her for the eyelash curler, she knew exactly what that was. She knew the names for blush and mascara and lip gloss, too, which I was not very interested in knowing.

However and nevertheless, I knew if I was going to be a fashion designer I would need someone to know the things I did not know. Elizabeth was going to be so **flattered** when I told her she was hired for a job she hadn't even applied for.

When my face was all disgusting with glop, it was time to move on to hair. I sat very still in the chair while Kevin put those gross flowers back in and twirled my hair around and pinned it. When he was done **planting a garden** on my head, it was time for me to change into my outfit.

My mom was getting her makeup

done now, and everyone else was rushing around trying to get ready.

I ran over to my station and hid behind a clothing rack so no one would see what I was doing. Right before I took the flowers out of my hair, I realized something very important: It wasn't just that I didn't like having flowers in my hair, **I didn't like having hair that people wanted to put flowers in!** I needed to do something about that fact, fast.

I ran over to Elliott's station and asked if I could borrow the scissors, and Elliott said yes, which meant he was the boss of scissors.

When I got back to my station, Millicent was there reading. She didn't even look up. I took a lot of tissues and wiped off all the gross makeup. Then I took all the flowers and pins out of my hair and started to cut it. That's when Millicent looked up.

"What are you doing?" she asked.

"Cutting off my hair so no one ever plants trees and flowers in it."

"Let me see!" she said.

I turned to face her, and she studied me for a minute and then broke out into the biggest smile of ever.

"You look just like Penelope, a character in my favorite book! Could you give me the same haircut?" she asked.

"Okay, after I finish mine."

Then she stood there very patiently as I finished cutting my hair. We could hear Laura Munn yelling for everyone to line up, so I had to cut Millicent's hair very, very quickly. When I was done, she looked at herself in the mirror and fell in love with herself.

"Thank you, Frannie," she said. "I love it."

Then I rushed over to my garment bag and unzipped it, and when Millicent saw my dress she gasped so loud **her mouth almost fell off her head**.

# CHAPTER

"Frannie!" Millicent cried. "Did you do that to your dress?"

I nodded, nervous that she hated it.

"Will you do that to mine?" she asked. I looked at her dress, and then we heard our names. Laura Munn was shouting for everyone to get in line.

"Three minutes, people! Three minutes! Models, take your places!"

"I don't think there's time, Millicent. I'm really sorry!" I told her.

I could tell she had a big **disappointment puddle** dropping at her feet.

"Maybe later," she said. "Come on, we have to go."

"You go first, okay? Tell them I'll be right there," I told Millicent, who ran out from behind the wardrobe rack where we were hiding.

I heard gasps and people shouting about her hair. I couldn't help but smile. I loved when I did things so well, people shouted about them.

Then I heard my mother's voice calling for me. Just as I was putting the other rain boot on my foot, the wardrobe rack I was hiding behind was pushed away. My mother stood there and saw me, and that's when everyone else saw me, too.

But no one's face went into an **excitified** smile. No one started clapping or yelling bravo for me. Instead there were bad gasps, and Elizabeth yelled in a very offendished way, "You wiped off all your makeup!"

And Kevin shouted, "Your hair! You chopped off your beautiful hair!"

And my mother yelled, "What did you do to yourself, Frances? What in the world did you do to that beautiful dress? And your hair? Your hair!"

Laura Munn hadn't said a word yet. When I looked up at her, she was holding her hand over her mouth, and her face was **berry-red**. That's when Millicent's mom started shouting at the other end of the room. When I looked over, she was shouting at Millicent, which gave me a really **bad day feeling** on my skin.

"Oh no! Frances, you didn't!" my

mother said, looking over at Millicent and Monica. Then my mom rushed over there and left me alone. That is when Laura Munn rushed toward me.

"I cannot believe you did this," Laura Munn said to me, with a very scary voice that told me I was in a **worldwide of trouble**. "I honestly can't believe this is happening to me right now!"

This was not at all the afterward that was supposed to occur. They were supposed to jump for joy, and they were not even close to jumping.

"I can't let you go onstage like this. Frannie, you're out of the show," Laura said in a not very friendly voice.

"But what about my mom?" I asked.

"Obviously she can't go alone, so she can't go onstage, either."

That is when I looked over at my

mother, who was still with Millicent and Monica. I could not believe how disappointed she was going to be. I had the worst day feeling on my skin.

Laura Munn rushed away from me and was clapping her hands off her arms and yelling, "Thirty seconds, people! Thirty seconds."

Julia, who was in the grade above me, wouldn't budge. She was crying, and she wouldn't get in line. My mom, Millicent, and Millicent's mom started to rush back over, and Laura was looking very upsettish about Julia. Even Julia's mom couldn't calm her down. Laura ran over to help calm Julia down and gave her assistant the job of shouting the seconds. Which she did extra **yellishly**.

"Ten seconds," the assistant

screamed at us. Julia was not budging.

"Five seconds!" the assistant screamed, very red in the face with an "I am very serious about shouting seconds at you" expression.

My mom was already in line, and she was waving her hand at me really fast to tell me to come on. The music had already started, and Laura's assistant began giving gentle pushes to the first models, which meant they had to go on. Once they went, the line started moving really fast. Julia's arms were crossed, and she was shaking her head no!

That's when I decided I had to take Julia's place. I ran toward my mom and took her hand. Before I could even breathe, Laura's assistant put her hand on my mom's and my backs and yelled, *"Go!"*

I did not like being yelled at, and I did not like that Laura took us out of the show, and I did not like how terrible I made my mom feel. **I was in a very bad day kind of mood.**

My mom started down the catwalk. I was supposed to count to five before following behind her, which I did. I was

so **upsettish** at everything that had happened, I wasn't even nervous about being on the runway. I didn't even want to be on the runway. And that is a for instance of why I stomped down the stage past my mom in the maddest mad I'd ever felt before in my life. I did not even smile, not once, and when I got to

the end of the stage, I was glad I wasn't supposed to stand for longer than three seconds.

I did not want to be a model, not one bit at all. I wanted to be a fashion designer, and not one person backstage told me how amazing the dress was. Instead they got mad at me! I turned around the second I got to the end of the stage, and I stormed all the way back. The clapping grew really loud when I left the stage, which meant that everyone was really glad I was gone. *See*, I thought to myself and everyone else, *I am a bad model!* I should never have been a model in the first place! I should only have been a fashion designer, but no one even appreciates my designs! I was very **upsettish**.

When I got backstage, I waited for

my mother to yell my entire face off, but she was talking to a woman who looked even more **upsettish** than me! When they both started to walk in my direction, I got a very bad day feeling in my belly.

"Frances," my mother said when they reached me. "I'd like you to meet Nora Kelly—the woman who designed the dress you are wearing."

When I looked at Nora Kelly, I could tell she was not happy at all about what I did to her dress, which left me a little **confusified**. I thought I had made it better. I made it more like me! Wasn't that the point of clothing? To make it match the person who wears it?

"Why did you do that to my dress?" Nora asked me with a voice that was very shaky.

"I . . . I . . . " I looked down at my feet. I suddenly felt very ashamed. "I don't like flowers," I told her.

"Well, I like flowers! That is why I made the dress with flowers. I worked so hard on it, and it was an original."

When she said *original*, that's when I knew I'd done a really bad thing. I learned the hard way about originals. *Original* means one of a kind, which is a good thing if you're a person, but bad if you're a dress that's been **ruined**.

"I'm sorry," I told her. "I didn't mean to hurt your feelings."

"You didn't hurt my feelings," she said. "You hurt my dress." Then she stopped and looked like she was holding tears back into her eye sockets before she changed her mind and said, "Well, maybe you hurt my feelings a little bit."

This made me feel the most awful of any awful I've ever felt. I did not like to hurt the feelings of anyone, but especially not adult people. I didn't know how to fix adult people's hurt feelings. Even though I wanted to be an adult, I wasn't exactly sure what it was like to be an adult.

Just when I was about to try to say that I was really sorry, there was a bit of a commotion, and everyone turned to look at a big, **smiley-faced** woman carrying a poodle. When she saw me she shouted, "That's the one!" and started toward me. A couple of younger-looking people followed behind her. I did not know who these people were, but I was very afraid that I was about to be arrested.

I reached out and held my mother's

hand, and I think she thought I was going to be arrested also because she pulled me in closer to her. When the woman reached me she said, "Who made this dress?"

Nora Kelly looked at the woman, and suddenly, she grew very red and shiny in her face. "You're Anna Armstrong," Nora said.

"Yes, I am. Who are you?"

"I'm Nora Kelly. I designed this dress," she said.

"It's genius! Absolutely genius! How you crossed out all the flowers and hacked into it. I love the interplay between masculine and feminine. You've managed to design something with a message. It's wonderful. And the galoshes! *J'adore!*" the woman cried, clapping her hands together. That is when Nora Kelly's face dropped.

"And the lack of makeup and the chopped off hair. Who was the stylist on this? It's absolutely fabulous. This is the type of look I want to see on the runway next season. This is the next stage of fashion for adults. How in the world did you think this up?" Anna asked her.

That's when my mother, whose mouth was so wide with surprise, turned to me and looked really **shocktified**.

"I didn't," Nora Kelly admitted.

"You didn't?" Anna Armstrong was confused.

"I did," I said.

"You made the dress?" she asked.

"No. I just ruined it."

"Oh no, my child. You didn't ruin it.

You made it better," she said. "That is some talent you have inside you."

**My hidden talent!** I had it after all!

"It's absolutely marvelous. How did you ever think to cross out the flowers?"

"Well, Laura Munn said she was giving everyone dresses that matched who they were, and she gave me a flowered one, which is a for instance of something that doesn't match me at all. And that made me really offendish and mad, so I crossed out and cut off everything that didn't match me. Then I put on my galoshes because I love them and cut my hair short so they wouldn't put a flower garden in it. Also, I took off all the makeup because I didn't like to feel like I was wearing two faces at one time. And that is how I thought of it."

"It's just fabulous." Then she reached

into her bag, pulled out a business card, and handed it to my mother.

"I am the editor for *Fashionista Magazine*—"

*Fashionista Magazine?* Even I had heard of that. It was **very, very famous**.

"I'd love the chance to talk more with your daughter. Perhaps you can call me next week, and we can set up a meeting?" she asked my mom.

A meeting?! A meeting?! All I'd ever wanted in my entire life was to have a meeting.

"Well, she's in quite a bit of trouble, so we'll see."

"Well, perhaps you can punish her *and* take a meeting with me."

"Perhaps," my mom said.

"Perhaps always sounds like a yes to

my ears," she said, waving to us as she walked away. Nora's mouth was wide open as she watched Anna Armstrong leave.

Then she turned to me and said, "I can't believe it. I simply cannot believe it. I work for years and years to make beautiful clothing, then you come along, tear mine apart, and you're discovered!"

Then Nora started to cry. Her face got very red and blotchy. I felt the most **horrendimous** I had in years. I did not like to make people feel bad, certainly not adults, and I definitely did not like to make them cry. I did not know what I was supposed to do.

Laura Munn clapped her hands together and got everyone's attention.

"Thank you so much everyone for a very eventful fashion show. I think it was a real success, despite some surprising moments. To celebrate, Mrs. Pellington has brought a chocolate cake with strawberry filling and other sweets and surprises for all of you. So let's go down and celebrate in the cafeteria."

Everyone started to hurry toward the cafeteria, and I followed, but my mother reached out and grabbed my hand.

"I don't think so, Frannie."

"Why not? You love cake!" I reminded her in case she forgot.

"I know I love cake. You love cake, too. But I don't see any reason for you to be rewarded right now. You destroyed someone else's property. How would you like it if someone ruined something you put all your heart and soul into making?"

"But I made it more my style, and a

magazine liked it! I made it better!"

"No, you made it to suit your taste. Your taste is not everyone else's taste, Frannie. Nora did not make this dress just for you. She made it because it meant something to her. You need to learn how to appreciate things that may not suit your taste."

I scrunched up my face at this sentence. Why would a person want to appreciate something that was not their taste?

"Millicent! Monica!" my mom called to them as they headed out the door toward the cafeteria. "Can you wait for a second, please? Frannie has something she wants to say to you."

We walked over to Millicent and Monica, and I said to Monica, "I am very sorry that I ruined your life by cutting off Millicent's hair."

"You didn't ruin my life, Frannie, but you should have asked my permission. Even **professional** stylists know they have my permission before they cut Millicent's hair."

"They do?" I asked.

"Of course. You need to think a bit more before you act," she told me.

Monica accepted my apology, and they left to get some cake.

I stared at my still-very-mad mom. "Let's go meet your father," she said. "We need to decide what your consequences will be."

That sentence gave me a very bad day feeling on my skin.

# CHAPTER

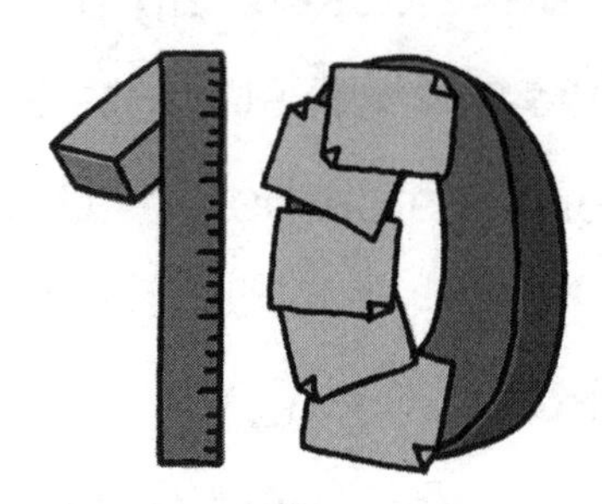

My father was very disappointed in me, which felt **twenty-fourteen** times worse than making Nora Kelly upset. I had to stay in my room while he and my mom had a conversation about my punishment, which I knew was going to be very bad. I thought about the absolute worst things they could punish me with so that whatever punishment they decided on wouldn't feel so **tragical**.

One punishment that would be very terrible would be if they made me live with Nora Kelly for the rest of my life.

Another one that would be really bad would be if they sent me to live in Atlanta, which is a city I've heard of that is nowhere near Chester, New York.

Another terrible idea would be if they made me sleep on the basement floor for the rest of my life. Without blankets or a pillow or even a night-light.

Those were three really horrendimous things they could punish me with. As long as I didn't have to live with Nora Kelly, move to another city, or sleep all by myself in the basement without blankets for the rest of my life, I would feel amazing with whatever punishment they gave me.

I almost jumped out of my skin suit

when they knocked on my door.

My parents came in with smiles that said they were very happy with the punishment they made up.

My mom sat on my bed, I sat next to her, and my dad stood with his hands on his hips.

"Frances, I want you to know that we are both extremely disappointed."

"I know," I told him. "I am horrendimously sorry."

"What I don't understand is why you would ruin someone else's hard work. That doesn't seem to be in character with who you are," my dad said.

Character is a really adult thing that my dad and I sometimes talk about. The kind of character he was discussing had to do with the person you are on the inside, not the cartoon type. A for instance of what I mean is, if you are a helpful person, then you act helpful when people need you. But if you act unhelpful when people need you, then you are not being who you say you are, which is a helpful person!

"You mean because I am a person who doesn't normally ruin other people's hard work?"

"That's exactly what I mean," he said.

"We just don't understand why you would do that. Were you angry?"

I stood up. "Yes! I was! I was very angrified!" I said, very **relieviated** that they put the right word to the feeling I had.

"What were you so angry about?" my dad wanted to know.

"Laura Munn said she was going to match the dress to our personalities, and I was very offendified at the dress she thought was my personality!" I told them.

"When you think about it now, was cutting up the dress and drawing on it the right response?" my dad asked me.

I sat back down because I had to think about that. What I thought was this: Probably not.

"Probably not," I said out loud.

"And what would have been the right response?" my mom asked.

I thought about that, too. When I actually thought about all their questions I started to feel very **ashamified** of myself. I knew better than to cut and draw on someone else's property. Why did I do that? Maybe I did it because I wasn't thinking about these questions. I was only thinking about my **offendified** feelings.

"Maybe to say something with my voice, out loud to someone?"

"Like what?" my dad asked.

"Like, 'I do not prefer this dress

because I do not think it matches who I am.'"

"Maybe you could have asked Laura Munn why she thought the dress matched your personality. Maybe her answer would have made sense to you, and you would have been flattered. Instead, you made up your own answers and took things into your own hands and made things much, much worse."

I had never even thought about asking Laura **a why type** of question.

"Maybe we should call Laura and ask her why she thought that dress matched you," my mother offered.

That was a really good idea. My mom looked up Laura's number and wrote it down for me.

"I have a phone call to make myself, actually," my mom said.

"We'll be back in a couple of minutes," my dad told me as I turned to dial Laura Munn's phone number. When it started to ring, moths and butterflies filled up my entire belly.

"Laura Munn," she answered. I had never heard anyone answer the phone like that before.

"Hi, Laura Munn. This is Frances B. Miller. I'm the girl who ruined the dress and maybe even your life," I said.

"I know who you are, Frannie. What can I do for you?"

"Well, I wondered if I could ask you a question."

"Of course. Ask away."

"Why did you match that flowery dress with me?"

"I was wondering when you were going to ask me that," Laura Munn said to my shocktified ears.

"You were?" I asked. "I didn't know about that fact."

"I wanted you to wear that dress, Frannie, because seeing a tomboy in a flowery dress is unexpected and surprising. Just like you."

"I am unexpected and surprising?" I asked. This was very interesting to me.

"Yes. I've never met a little girl who carries a briefcase before—"

"I also have a résumé and business cards," I interrupted.

"You are one of a kind, Frannie. I liked the idea of putting such a serious, ambitious girl in a lighthearted dress. It's an opposite, and I like opposites."

"I like opposites, too!" I told her. Which is not an opinion. I do like opposites, even if I didn't know about that fact until right then.

"I'm glad you understand," she said.

"I do. I'm sorry if I ruined your life, Laura Munn," I told her.

She laughed at that, but not in a bad way.

"You didn't ruin my life, Frannie. But you did put me in a very bad position. You didn't think about how your actions might affect other people, did you?"

"No, I didn't."

"Well, I hope you learned an important lesson," she said. "You're not going to like everything in life, but you are going to have to learn how to accept things without cutting up dresses."

"I know," I told her.

"Good. I have a meeting, Frannie, so I have to run, but thanks for calling and asking about the dress."

"You are very welcome," I told her.

I felt a **hundredy** times better. It wasn't a bad reason she gave me the dress, it was a good reason! I couldn't even believe my worldwide ears. That's when I got a very bad day feeling on my skin. I really did a bad thing by cutting up Nora Kelly's dress. That is when my parents walked back into my room.

# CHAPTER 11

"We have the perfect punishment for you," my mom told me. I did not like how **happy** they seemed about having a punishment for me.

"You are going to spend a day with Nora Kelly doing one of her favorite activities."

"Okay," I said. That didn't sound so bad. I loved favorite activities.

"Flower arranging," my dad finished.

I stood up. “Flower arranging?!” I cried. “I am not interested in flowers or in flower arranging!” I said.

“We know. That’s exactly why you are going to join her. You need to learn how to appreciate things that are not your style.”

I **harrumphed** my face at this fact and at this punishment. Flower arranging was the most boringest thing in the world. I would rather go to jail than go to flower arranging.

“She’ll pick you up on Saturday morning, and you’ll spend the entire day with her. When we pick you up, we would like to hear three things about flower arranging that you genuinely liked. We would also like to hear three things you can appreciate about flower arranging, even if you didn't like those specific things."

I scrunched up my face at this. I did not like being given homework by my parents!

"Fine. I will do that, but I will not like it at all."

"You don't need to like it," my dad said. "You just need to appreciate it."

And so that is what I had to do. On Saturday morning, Nora Kelly drove to my house and picked me up for the most worst activity in the world. I did not know how in the whole wide world of America I was going to come up with *three* things I appreciated about flower arranging. But when Nora told me the class was at a flower shop, I thought that sounded a little bit exciting. I liked the idea of having a class in a real-life business place.

When we got there, there were a lot of adults, which made me feel like I was doing a grown-up thing. The teacher was named Todd. He was so excited about flowers that I couldn't help but get a little excited, too. Would you even believe your ears if I told you that flower arranging was an art? **That's a scientific fact!**

The flower store also had cactus plants, which is a for instance of

something I didn't know I loved.

We made big arrangements out of lots of flowers and small arrangements out of a few flowers.

When my parents got there, I thought they were extremely early, but they were actually on time. That is how fast the time went, actually. I showed them all around the store and explained about flower arranging.

"Seems like you had a good time," my dad said, holding my hand.

"I really did," I told him.

My parents looked at each other and smiled. Then they looked at me.

"Did you manage to find three things about flower arranging that you appreciated?" my dad asked me.

I nodded my head.

"I liked learning about all the flowers and the ways they grow. I liked being in a class with adults. I liked how many colors there were. I liked learning thirty-seventeen different names of flowers. I liked Todd, the teacher. I liked doing something with Nora. I liked being the boss of my own vase. I liked learning how to take care of something. Is that three?" I asked.

"I think that's around eight, actually," my dad said.

"We're so glad you learned to like something you thought you wouldn't like, Frannie."

"Me too," I said. "Sometimes you don't know what you'll like until you try it!" I told them.

"So true!" my dad said, taking my hand. Then I looked at them and said to my mom, "I was hoping we could go to that meeting with Anna Armstrong."

"I don't know, Frannie," she said, hesitating.

"I want Nora to come with us. I couldn't have ruined her dress if she hadn't made it. So we're a team, actually. I wouldn't feel right going without her," I said.

My mom took my hand and said, "Seems like you learned quite a lot today, Frannie. You've got yourself a deal."

I told Nora the good news. She could hardly believe her **ear sockets**! I smiled the biggest smile ever knowing that I hadn't only helped Nora, but also made her happy.

**THE END.**

# Want more Frannie?